Robert Neubecker

LINUS THE VEGETARIAN T. REX

Beach Lane Books • New York London Toronto Sydney New Delhi

For Izzosaur and Josiraptor

BEACH LANE BOOKS
An imprint of Simon & Schuster Children's Publishing Division
1230 Avenue of the Americas, New York, New York 10020
Copyright © 2013 by Robert Neubecker
All rights reserved, including the right of reproduction in whole or in part in any form.
BEACH LANE BOOKS is a trademark of Simon & Schuster, Inc.
For information about special discounts for bulk purchases, please contact Simon & Schuster
Special Sales at 1-866-506-1949 or business@simonandschuster.com.
The Simon & Schuster Speakers Bureau can bring authors to your live event.
For more information or to book an event, contact the Simon & Schuster Speakers Bureau
at 1-866-248-3049 or visit our website at www.simonspeakers.com.
Book design by Lauren Rille
The text for this book is set in Souvenir.
The illustrations for this book are rendered in India ink on Arches watercolor paper,
and colored on a Macintosh computer with fingerprints and collage.
Manufactured in China
0413 SCP
First Edition
10 9 8 7 6 5 4 3 2 1
Library of Congress Cataloging-in-Publication Data
Neubecker, Robert.
Linus the vegetarian *T. rex* / Robert Neubecker.—1st ed.
p. cm.
Summary: Ruth Ann MacKenzie, who loves natural history, eagerly enters a new museum exhibit
called Cretaceous Surprises where she meets a most unusual *Tyrannosaurus rex*.
ISBN 978-1-4169-8512-9 (hardcover)
ISBN 978-1-4424-8187-9 (eBook)
[1. *Tyrannosaurus rex*—Fiction. 2. Dinosaurs—Fiction. 3. Vegetarianism—Fiction.
4. Museums—Fiction.] I. Title.
PZ7.N4394Lin 2013
[E]—dc23
2012018190

Special thanks to Andrea Welch, Lauren Rille, Linda Pratt,
and the rest of the museum staff.

Ruth Ann MacKenzie was a member of the Museum of Natural History, and she had a membership card to prove it.
Ruth Ann *loved* natural history.

She knew all about the Ice Age.

She knew all about the oceans.

But what did Ruth Ann know the *most* about?

TYRANNOSAURUS REX

THE DINOSAURS!

She knew their names.

She knew when they lived.

And she *definitely* knew what they ate.

So when the Cretaceous Surprises exhibit opened,
she didn't expect to be surprised.

But she was!

"HELLO, I'M LINUS!"

said a gigantic *Tyrannosaurus rex*.
"Please don't eat me!" cried Ruth Ann.
"Eat you? Oh my heavens, no. I wouldn't
dream of it!" said Linus. "I *am* quite
hungry, though. Won't you join
me for lunch?"

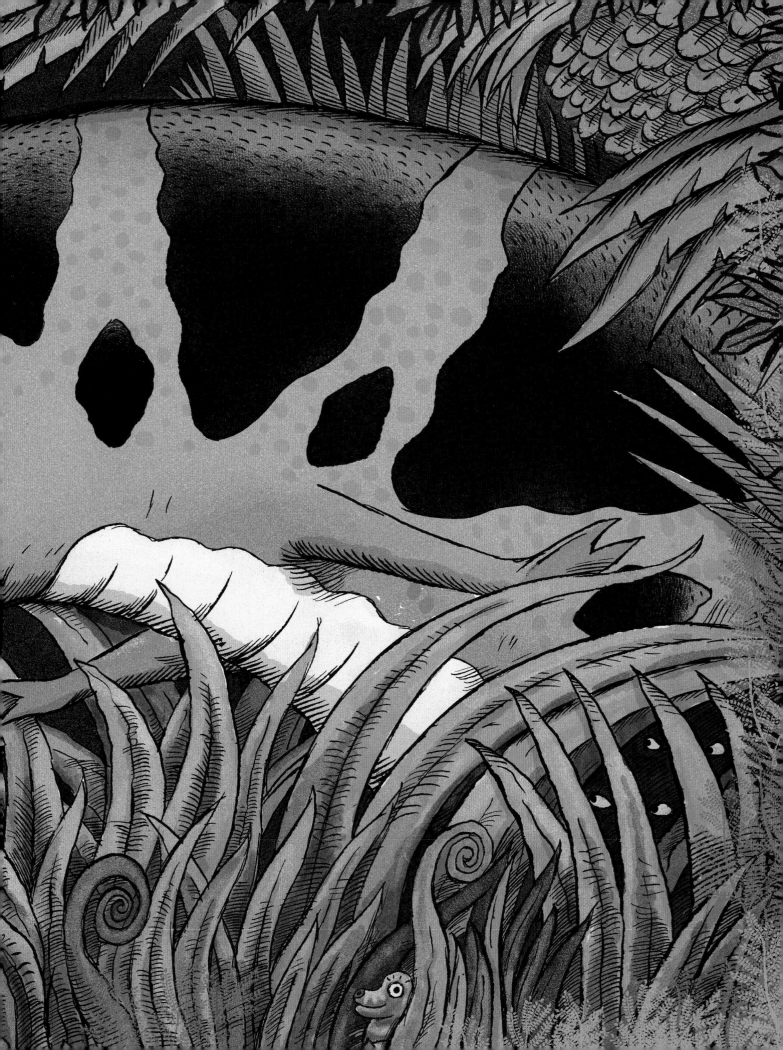

"Um, what's on the menu?" asked Ruth Ann.
"That depends," said Linus. "Let's go hunting!"

First Linus attacked . . .

a patch of arugula!

Then he cornered . . .

Next Linus stalked . . .

some yummy broccoli.

Then he pounced . . .

on a plump tomato!

When Linus greeted a herd of iguanodons, Ruth Ann couldn't stand it any longer.

"Didn't you want to eat those guys?"
asked Ruth Ann.
"I wouldn't dream of it," said Linus.
"They're my friends!"

"Your *friends*?" asked Ruth Ann.
"Linus, don't you know what kind
of dinosaur you are?"
"Why, of course," said Linus.

"But, Linus," said Ruth Ann,
"you're a *T. rex*!
   You're supposed to be a predator!
   You're supposed to be fierce!
   You're supposed to be—"

"Velociraptors!"

interrupted Linus.

He grabbed Ruth Ann and set her at
the top of the tallest tree.
Then he turned around and . . .

ROARED
AND
ROARED
AND
ROARED!

The velociraptors ran away so fast,
it was like they had never been there at all.

"Was *that* fierce enough for you?" asked Linus.
"Fierce? That was *ferocious*. You're my hero, Linus!"
said Ruth Ann.

"Nonsense!" said Linus. "I'm just me—a very big, very brave, very **VEGETARIAN** *Tyrannosaurus rex!*"

Linus and Ruth Ann spent the afternoon munching on veggies and chatting about all things Cretaceous.

Then it was time to say good-bye.
Ruth Ann stepped through the curtain . . .

and found herself back in the museum.

She had enough time for one more exhibit.
But now she wasn't sure what to expect.

The museum was *full* of surprises.